WHY MOLE SHOUTED
and Other Stories

LORE SEGAL

Pictures by SERGIO RUZZIER

Frances Foster Books • Farrar, Straus and Giroux • New York

The author wants to thank W. D. Snodgrass
for his help with rhyming

Text copyright © 2004 by Lore Segal
Pictures copyright © 2004 by Sergio Ruzzier
All rights reserved
Distributed in Canada by Douglas & McIntyre Ltd.
Color separations by Hong Kong Scanner Arts
Printed and bound in the United States of America by Berryville Graphics
Designed by Barbara Grzeslo
First edition, 2004
1 3 5 7 9 10 8 6 4 2

Library of Congress Cataloging-in-Publication Data
Segal, Lore Groszmann.
    Why Mole shouted and other stories / Lore Segal ; pictures by Sergio Ruzzier.
        p.   cm.
    Summary: Young Mole and his grandmother live together and get along well
enough most of the time, but in each of these four stories there is an exception to
the rule.
    Contents: When Mole lost his glasses — When Mole wouldn't zip his jacket
— Why Mole shouted — Why Mole asked why.
    ISBN 0-374-38417-7
    [1. Moles (Animals)—Fiction.   2. Grandmothers—Fiction.   3. Behavior—
Fiction.]   I. Ruzzier, Sergio, ill.   II. Title.

PZ7.S4527 Wh 2004
[Fic]—dc21
                                                                    2002026438

To Grandmother's two best Moles
Benjamin
Isaiah
—L.S.

For my mother, Carolina, and my daughter, Viola
—S.R.

WHEN MOLE LOST HIS GLASSES
Chapter 1

Once there was a Mole. He lived with his Grandmother Mole, and they would have got on well enough if he had only remembered to always put things back where they belonged.

Now moles—you may or may not know this—can't see until they put their glasses on. In the morning Mole opened his eyes, sat up in bed and patted his pillow on the right side, the left side. He patted his blanket. He patted the floor next to his bed.

"Grandmother Mole," he said, "I can't find my glasses."

Grandmother Mole said, "Where did you put them?"

"Oh, Grandmother *Mole*!" said Mole. "If I knew that, wouldn't I take them and put them on my nose?"

Grandmother Mole sighed a sigh Mole couldn't miss. She said, "You're sitting on them, and they're all bent out of shape. Give them here."

Grandmother Mole fixed Mole's glasses and said, "You have to pick a place where your glasses belong and always remember to put them back there."

Mole said, "I'm going to put my glasses on the little table next to my bed, and when I need them, that's where they are going to be."

Grandmother Mole said, "I have things I have to do. I'm going out. Be my good Mole and always put things back where they belong."

Then she kissed him on the nose and went on her way.

By the time Grandmother Mole got home, Mole had lost his glasses again. He said, "I can't find them."

Grandmother Mole said, "Look on the little table next to your bed."

Mole said, "They aren't there."

Grandmother Mole said, "Where did you put them?"

"Oh, Grandmother *Mole*!" said Mole.

Grandmother Mole said, "You have to retrace your steps: When was the last time you remember having your glasses on your nose?"

"When you kissed it, before you went to do the things you had to do."

Grandmother Mole said, "What did you do after I went out?"

Mole said, "I stood on my head."

"Do you remember taking off your glasses?"

"I remember being upside down," said Mole.

"What did you do next?"

"I was hungry and went looking for a chocolate chip cookie."

"Do you remember if you were wearing your glasses?" Grandmother Mole asked him.

Mole said, "What I remember is not finding any cookies."

"What did you do after that?"

"I was sleepy and took a nap."

Grandmother Mole said, "I know where your glasses are. Go and look in your bed. I bet you were lying on them!"

Mole couldn't miss the sigh that Grandmother Mole sighed. She said, "Give them here. I'll straighten them out for you."

Mole said, "How I wish that when I take my glasses off my nose I would always remember to put them on my bedside table, because until I put my glasses on I can't see, and when I can't see I can't find my glasses."

"Here you are," said Grandmother Mole. "I've fixed them."

Mole put on his glasses and kissed his grandmother and said, "You are my good Grandmother Mole."

"And you are my dear Mole," said Grandmother Mole, "even if you're never going to remember to put anything back where it belongs."

WHEN MOLE WOULDN'T ZIP HIS JACKET
Chapter 1

Once there was a Mole who lived with his Grandmother Mole in a hole in the forest.

Now you may or may not know that moles wear thick fur jackets. "Zip it all the way up," Grandmother Mole said to Mole. "I don't want you catching cold and coming home coughing and sneezing. Why don't you stay inside where it's nice and warm."

"It's not so cold out," Mole said.

"Oh, yes it is," said Grandmother Mole.

"No, it is *not*," Mole said.

"It is *too*," said Grandmother Mole. "It is very, very cold, and windy. Look! It's snowing."

"That's why I want to go out and play with Little Gopher," said Mole. "We want to scoot around in the snow and throw snowballs and make a great big snow mole!"

"Well, then," Grandmother Mole said, "I'll make you a nice, thick, hot cup of soup so you'll be fortified."

"Oh, for goodness' *sake*, Grandmother Mole!" said Mole.

"At least let me wrap my woolly scarf around your throat. And put on your gloves! Pull your cap all the way down and zip the zipper all the way up!"

When Mole had gone out, Grandmother Mole went to the
cupboard, took out her woolly sweater and put it on, and
buttoned the buttons all the way up. She put a log on the fire.

Chapter 2

Mole and Little Gopher scooted around in the snow. They took off their gloves so they could make bigger, rounder snowballs to throw at each other. They built a snow mole and tied Grandmother's woolly scarf around its throat. Mole put his cap on the snow mole's head and pulled it way down over where the snow mole didn't have ears, because moles—you may or may not know this—have their ears on the inside.

When Mole got home, Grandmother Mole was lying in bed, and she was coughing and sneezing. She said, "I told you not to go out in the wind and snow!"

"Poor Grandmother Mole," said Mole, "you have a cold!" He put another log on the fire and warmed up a nice, thick, hot cup of soup for her and said, "This will make you feel better."

"You are the best Mole," Grandmother Mole said to him. "If only you would zip the zipper of your jacket all the way up!"

WHY MOLE SHOUTED

There once was a Mole who lived with his grandmother. Grandmother Mole loved her Mole very dearly except when he shouted. One day he started shouting, and he shouted and shouted and wouldn't stop.

"Please don't shout like that!" she told him.

"Aooooooooooooooo!" shouted Mole.

Grandmother Mole covered her head with her paws, but Mole kept shouting and shouting. "Aooooooooooo!" he shouted. "AoOOOOOOOOOOO, AOOOOOOOOO, and **AOOOOOOOOOOOOOO!**" He would not and would not stop.

"Why are you making such a terrible noise?" his grandmother asked him. "Why? WHY? **WHY?**"

"**AOOOOOOOOOOO!**" answered Mole at the top of his voice.

"I'll make you a deal," Grandmother Mole said to him. "If I guess the reason you are shouting, will you promise to stop?"

"Okay," agreed Mole.

"Okay," said Grandmother Mole. "Are you shouting because you are hungry?"

"**Aoooooooooooooooooo!**" shouted Mole.

So that wasn't it. "Thirsty?" Grandmother Mole asked him.

"**Aooooooooooooooooo!**"

"You're not thirsty. Sleepy?"

"Aoooooooooooooooooo!"

"Not sleepy. Is it that you're a sad Mole today?"

"Aoooooooooooooooooo!"

No. Mole wasn't hungry or thirsty. He wasn't sleepy. He wasn't sad.

"I know," Mole's Grandmother Mole said, "you mean, 'Notice me!'"

"Aooo . . ." began Mole, but he was thinking about it. "Ao?" he asked himself. "Oh!" he told himself, and stopped shouting.

Why Mole Asked Why

or

I'm a Poet and I Didn't Know It

There was once a Mole. Mole and his Grandmother Mole lived in a hole in the forest. One day he asked her why.

Grandmother Mole, who was setting the supper table, stopped and thought about it for a bit. She said,

"Because we're moles
and moles live in holes."

"Why?" Mole asked her.

Grandmother put out a plate for Mole, a plate for herself. She said,

"Because while you are sleeping, a beast might come creeping in the night, and (at the very least) take a bite."

"Why?" Mole asked her.

"Because," Grandmother Mole answered, "that's what this beast does."

"Why?" Mole asked her.

Grandmother Mole laid a knife and fork beside each plate. She said,

"Because he's a gourmet. He would take you into the forest, and make you into a pâté, or a mole cake, or (at the very wor-est) a mole soufflé to eat for a Sunday treat."

"Why?" Mole asked her.

"Because," Grandmother said, "you're sweet enough to eat. Now go get the serviettes."

"Why?" Mole asked her.

Grandmother said, "We're having ants vinaigrette."

"Why?" Mole asked her.

Grandmother answered, "Sometimes, the reason is it rhymes."

This time Mole made no reply.

Grandmother Mole thought perhaps she hadn't heard, and said, "Did you ask me why?"

Mole answered, "No! Not I!"

"Why?" Grandmother Mole asked him.

Mole held up both his paws. He said,

"Because."

The End